BOOGIE'S BIG IDEA
THE POOL PARTY

Dogbud Press

ISBN- 978-0-9986252-0-1

Dogbud Press

Boogie's Big Idea
The Pool Party

WRITTEN BY
CATHERINE GARDINER

iLLUSTRATED BY
ROSEMARIE GILLEN

Dogbud Press

Dedicated to dog lovers everywhere.
Read and enjoy!

"We're going to have a long day at work," said Mommy. "Be good doggies. There is plenty of water and you can play out in the backyard."

"See you this evening," Daddy pointed at Boogie, "please stay out of trouble!"

I'm bored,
thought Boogie.

Mama Wiggs glanced
around thinking, it's
too quiet when
Mommy and Daddy
are gone.

Z-z-z z-z z-z.

Petey snored
peacefully.

Boogie's ears perked up, "I have an idea!"

Uh-oh, Mama Wiggs rolled her eyes, Boogie always has big ideas.

"Petey, wake up!" Boogie barked. "Let's have a party!"

Climbing down, Petey yawned. "That sounds like fun."

Boogie bounced excitedly. "I know, right?"

"What can I do to help?" asked Mama Wiggs.
"I'll send the invitations!" Petey volunteered.

"I'll tidy things up and get some snacks," said Boogie, filling the dog's bowls with goodies.

"I'll carry some treats outside," offered Mama Wiggs.

"I'll fill the pool up," said Petey.

"Almost ready!" announced Mama Wiggs, gathering up their best toys for their guests.

"Everyone will be here soon," grinned Petey.

Boogie pranced back and forth. "I'm so excited!"

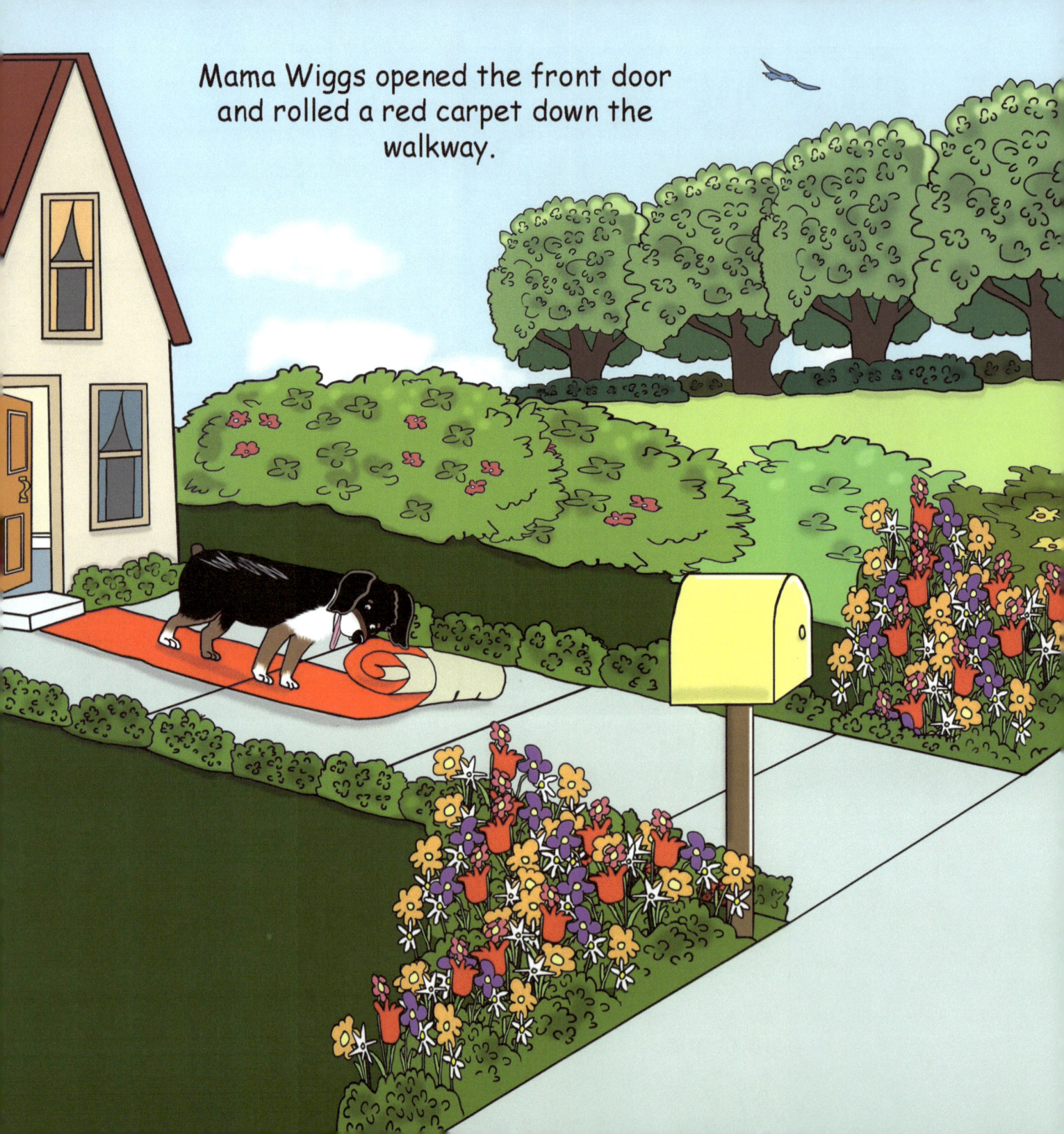

Mama Wiggs opened the front door and rolled a red carpet down the walkway.

"Look who's here, boys," said Mama Wiggs. "It's our ol' buddy, Vince."

Vince tipped his sunglasses. "Hi-ya fellas," he said. "Good to see ya."

"Vince agreed to be our door greeter," said Petey.

"Oh, I see," said Boogie, "that must be why
you're a bit early!"

Soon the party-goers began to stream up the walkway. Winnie and Greta pranced gingerly up to Vince.

"Good afternoon Ladies," he said.

The girls giggled.

"You may go right through and into the backyard," Vince instructed.

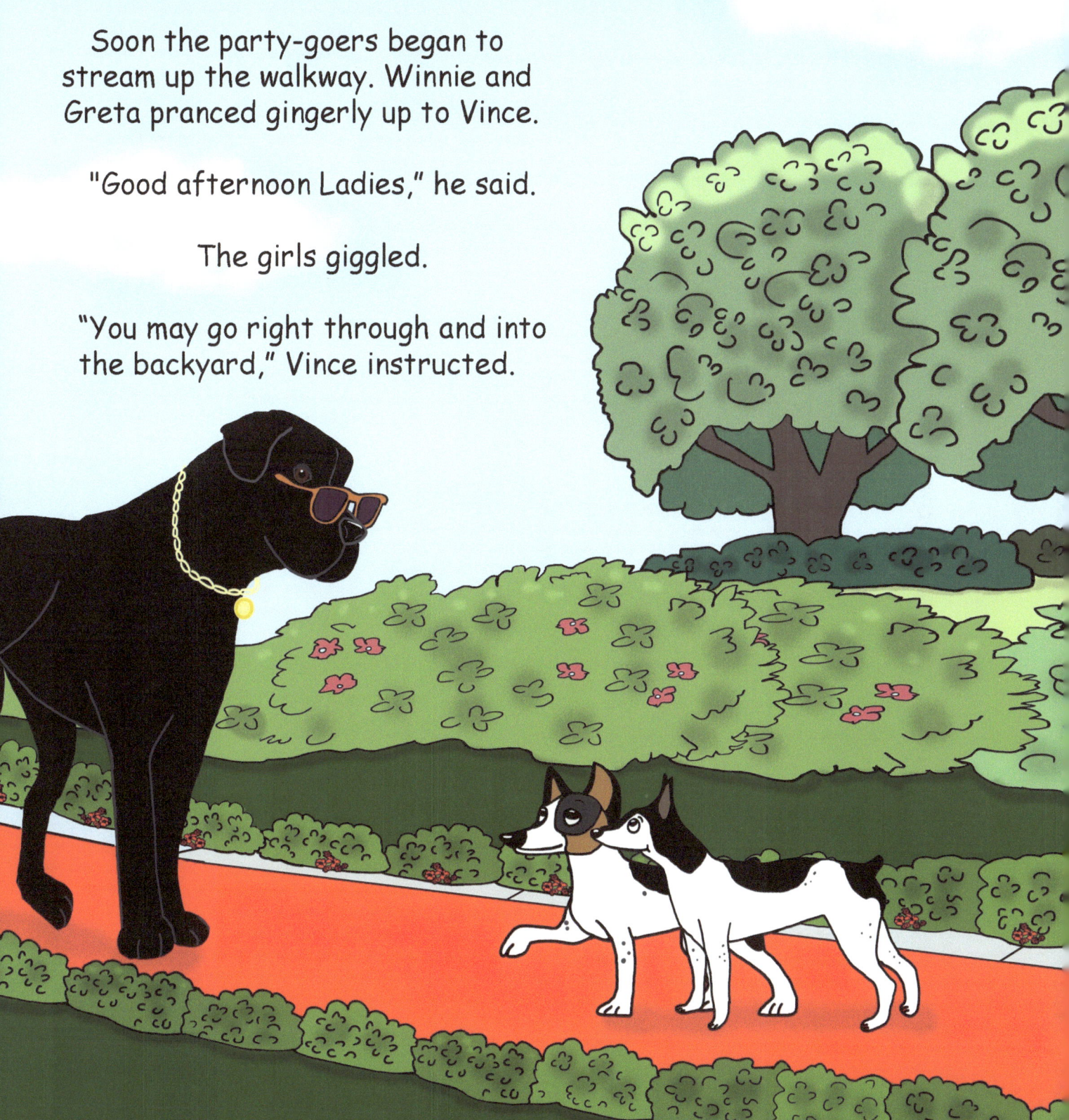

"I hope there'll be snacks," Molly smacked her lips in anticipation.

Boomer bounded towards the entrance, almost knocking Vince over.

Camille scampered right past Vince and yipped, "I can't wait to play with my friends!"

The party was hopping.

"Hey Boogie," yelled Winnie, "turn up the tunes!"

Boogie reached for the radio.

"Bombs away!" shouted Petey.

Friends kept coming. Poppa Bear hobbled to the front door.
"Never one to miss a good party!" he exclaimed.

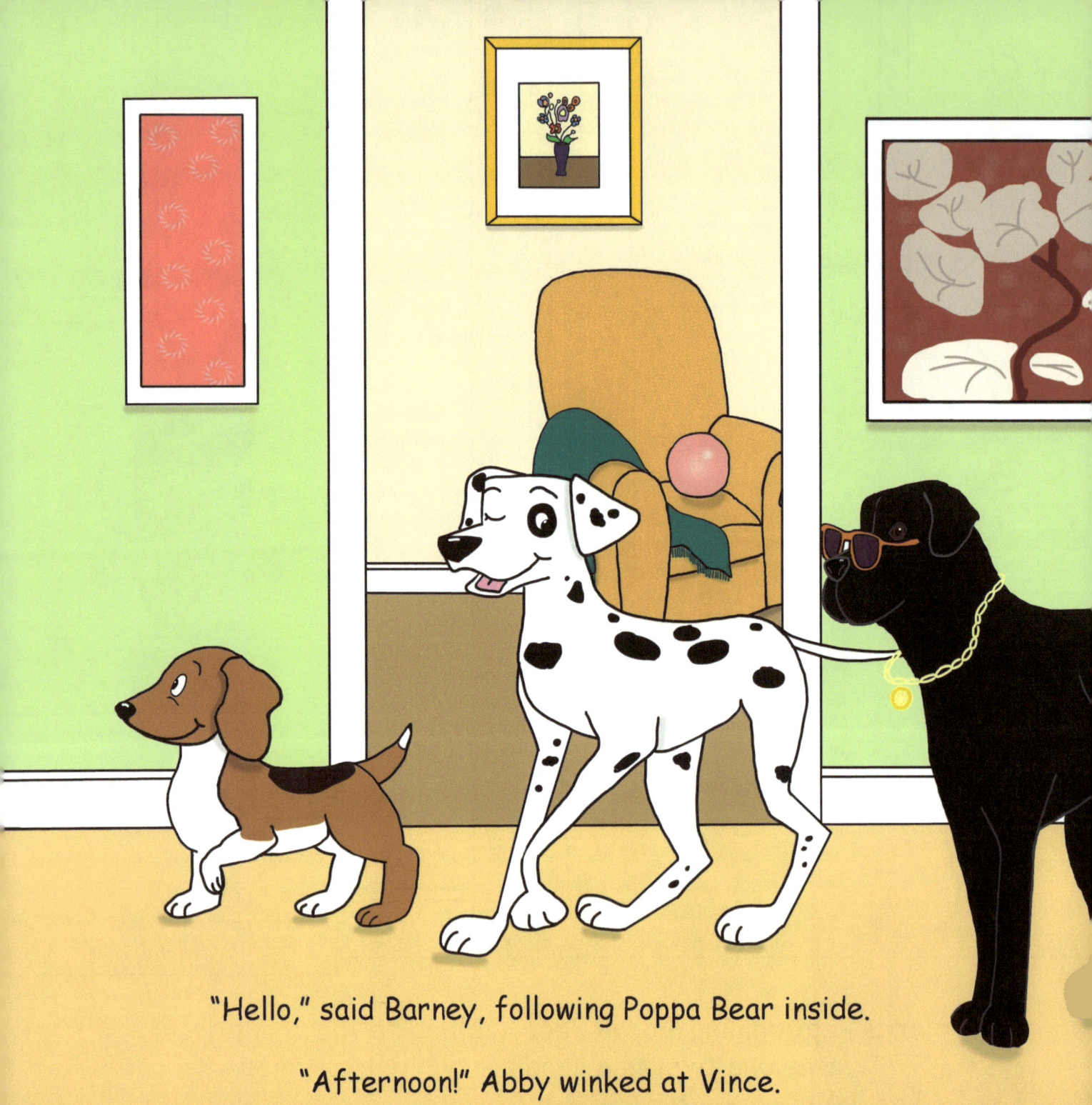

"Hello," said Barney, following Poppa Bear inside.

"Afternoon!" Abby winked at Vince.

Jasper, Jake and Charley were the last to arrive.

"Outta my way," ordered Jasper.

"Hey, no cutting the line!" shouted Jake.

"Woo-hoo!" howled Charlie, "point me to the backyard!"

Taking one last look down the red carpet, Vince prepared to close the door. Much to his surprise, he saw a dirty little pup, shyly limping towards him.

"Can I come in for a drink and a cookie?" begged the little pup.

"Where did you come from?" asked Vince.

"I'm homeless," the pup trembled. "I won't be any trouble, I promise!"

"Mama Wiggs?" Vince called out. "Would you come over here? We have an unexpected visitor."

Mama Wiggs looked down at the pitiful pup. "Did you receive an invitation?" she asked.

"No. I'm sorry." The pup dropped his head in shame.

Mama Wiggs sighed, then smiled warmly. "Don't just stand there, come inside and join us! We have plenty of treats to share."

"This turned out to be a great party," Petey said proudly. Grinning, he popped a munchie into his mouth.

Mama Wiggs tapped her toes to the music. "Everyone's having a terrific time!"

"The pool is a big hit too," added Boogie.

Petey yawned, "I think I'm ready for a snooze."

"More like a siesta," Mama Wiggs stretched. "I think I'll join you."

""I'll just chill right here in the pool," Boogie wiggled his toes in the water and began to drool.

It was getting late and the guests began to head for home. "Thanks for coming," said Petey, as Greta and Winnie pranced out the door.

"The snacks were de-lish!" said Molly," smacking her lips with delight.

Boomer hurried out. "Gotta chase squirrels!"

"Nice to see you, Barney" said Mama Wiggs.

"I had a wonderful time," said Barney.

"Me too!" agreed Poppa Bear, chewing on a tasty treat.

Abby nodded towards Mama Wiggs, "Have a good evening."

"Outta my way," ordered Jasper.

"Hey, no cutting the line!" shouted Jake.

"Woo-hoo!" howled Charlie, "that was the BEST PARTY EVER!"

"Nice to see you, Camille," said Petey.

"Thanks for the invite, a lovely party!" said Camille.

The last to leave, Vince howled with happiness. "My friends, that was one swingin' wingding! Ciao baby!"

Mama Wiggs glanced around thinking, it's too quiet now that everybody's gone.

Boogies' ears perked up, "I have an idea!"

Mama Wiggs rolled her eyes, "Boogie, what's your big idea this time?"

"Let's clean up together!" Boogie barked. "I'll pick up the toys."

Petey agreed. "I'll empty the pool."

"I'll roll up the red carpet," said Mama Wiggs, "and tidy the kitchen."

Mama Wiggs barked, "Good job everybody!"

Petey eyed the couch, "I'm ready for a snooze."

"Hey guys," Boogie snapped, "who's that sleeping in my bed?"

"That's the poor homeless pup,"
answered Mama Wiggs.

"What are we going to do with him?"
Petey asked.

Boogie reminded them, "Mommy and Daddy
will be home soon."

Mama Wiggs smiled, "Now it's ME who has an idea!"

Petey was amazed. "You look completely different," he said.

The pup asked timidly, "Do I look okay?"

"Okay? My friend, you look great, but who are you?" asked Petey.

"My name is Zeus!" the tiny dog said proudly.

A dog is the only thing on earth that loves you more than you love yourself!

BRU-M-M-M-M!

"What's THAT?"
Zeus trembled and ran to Boogie's bed.

"It's the garage door rumbling. Mommy and Daddy are back," replied Mama Wiggs.

"Who?" Zeus squeezed his eyes tightly closed, hoping it made him invisible.

A dog is the only thing on earth that loves you more than you love yourself!

"Hello puppies!" said Mommy,
"I hope you had a good day!"

Daddy looked startled. "WHO is THAT?"

Mommy looked at Daddy. Daddy looked at Mommy.
They both stared at the four sleeping doggies.

thing on earth that
loves you more than
you love yourself!

"Okay, so where's our kisses?"
asked Mommy.

Everybody jumped up,
tails wagging.

Boogie winked at Petey.
Petey let out a joyful bark.

Mama Wiggs nuzzled Mommy's
hand, while Zeus peeked over
the edge of Boogies bed.

After everyone settled down, Petey whispered, "That party was a lot of fun, Boogie."

"It certainly was," Mama Wiggs sighed. She glanced up at Zeus, who was gently snoring, sound asleep on Mommy's lap.

"Boogie, I think your big idea was the best ever!"

Stay tuned for our next
adventure.......